No turning back.

Cody found a seat and sat down. He adjusted his book bag next to him.

"He's sitting down," a girl behind him whispered loudly.

She was talking about him.

The bus started with a groan then jerked forward and they were on their way. Cody waved weakly to his father and to his mother, who was hopping up and down outside in the parking lot.

They had taken such good care of him up till this point in his life, and now he didn't know what had gotten into them. Camp was a dangerous place filled with bears and poison ivy. All kinds of bad things could happen. His only experience with bears was Yogi and Boo Boo.

"His name's Cody," another girl whispered. Cody looked at the name tag that his mother had put on his backpack.

She had labeled everything. Even his underwear had little labels with his name ironed inside. That way if he didn't make it out alive at least his parents would get his underwear back.

OTHER PUFFIN BOOKS YOU MAY ENJOY

Cody Unplugged

Betsy Duffey

Illustrated by Ellen Thompson

PUFFIN BOOKS

PUFFIN BOOKS
Published by the Penguin Group
Penguin Putnam Books for Young Readers,
345 Hudson Street, New York, New York 10014, U.S.A.
Penguin Books Ltd, 27 Wrights Lane, London W8 5TZ, England
Penguin Books Australia Ltd, Ringwood, Victoria, Australia
Penguin Books Canada Ltd, 10 Alcorn Avenue, Toronto, Ontario, Canada M4V 3B2
Penguin Books (N.Z.) Ltd, 182-190 Wairau Road, Auckland 10, New Zealand

Penguin Books Ltd, Registered Offices: Harmondsworth, Middlesex, England

First published in the United States of America by Viking,
a division of Penguin Putnam Books for Young Readers, 1999
Published by Puffin Books,
a division of Penguin Putnam Books for Young Readers, 2001

1 3 5 7 9 10 8 6 4 2

Text copyright © Betsy Duffey, 1999
Illustrations copyright © Ellen Thompson, 1999
All rights reserved

THE LIBRARY OF CONGRESS HAS CATALOGED THE VIKING EDITION AS FOLLOWS:
Duffey, Betsy.
Cody unplugged / by Betsy Duffey ; illustrated by Ellen Thompson.
p. cm.
Summary: Concerned that his television and video habits have gotten out of hand,
Cody's parents send him to Camp Bear where he learns to
experience real life rather than virtual reality.
ISBN 0-670-88592-4
[1. Camping—Fiction.] I. Thompson, Ellen (Ellen M.), ill. II. Title.
PZ7.D876Cod 1999 [Fic]—dc21 98-53756 CIP AC

Puffin Books ISBN 0-14-131240-8

Printed in the United States of America

RL: 2.8

Contents

Chapter 1

Oomachucka Oomachucka

"Cody?"

No answer. Cody was watching a Road Runner cartoon. Wile E. Coyote was pushing a giant anvil up the side of a mountain.

"Cody!"

Still no answer.

Coyote had reached the top and was waiting for Road Runner to pass under the cliff. His arms were held out in front of him, ready to push the anvil over the side.

"Cody, can you hear me?" Cody's mother was going through the mail as she walked into the living room.

"What?" Cody said. He didn't take his eyes off the TV.

"Look at me when I talk to you."

"Just a minute, Mom," he said.

"Turn that thing off."

Cody held the channel changer up toward the TV as if he was going to turn it off, but he didn't push the button.

"One second." Road Runner was coming around the bend. The anvil moved toward the edge.

His mother took five quick steps to the TV and pushed the power button. Coyote disappeared in a sea of blackness.

"Mom!" Cody blinked. "What did you do that for? Now I won't know how it ends."

"It always ends the same way," she said. "Coyote pushes the anvil off the cliff. The cliff breaks off and falls below the anvil. Then the anvil falls on Coyote and squishes him."

"Then he gets up and walks away," Cody added. "That's the best part, and I missed it."

His mother frowned. "Well," she said, "I

think this came just in time." She held up a video and a letter.

"A movie?" Cody said hopefully.

She shook her head. "Camp Bear," she said. "It's a video and a brochure about camp."

"Camp what?"

"Camp Bear. It's where I went to summer camp every year when I was your age."

"Why do they call it Camp Bear?" Cody asked.

"Because it's on Bear Mountain."

"Oh great, so if you send me to this camp I might get eaten by a bear."

"Cody, no one has ever been eaten by a bear at Camp Bear."

"How do you know?" Cody said. "That's not something they would put in the video."

In his mind Cody imagined the video, a scene of wide-eyed campers running through the forest chased by a giant bear.

"I can't go to camp," Cody said. "I have things to do. Chip and I are planning to watch the *Simpsons* marathon tomorrow—twenty back-to-back episodes. Then Wednesday we're going to watch—"

"Oh Cody, it would be great to be away from the TV for a week. You could hike and swim . . ."

"Wait a minute. No TV?"

"Right. There's not even any electricity at all."

"No microwaves or stereos?"

"None."

"You're kidding. Computers?"

"None."

"Nintendo?"

She shook her head.

"No Nintendo? That's child abuse."

"Cody, your father and I are worried about you. You haven't been outside in a week."

"I have too. I got the mail yesterday."

"You're not getting any exercise."

"I am. I watched the *Rise and Shine* fitness show this morning."

"Cody, you only *watched* it. You never left

the sofa. Summer should be filled with out-door activity: swimming, running, soccer."

"Mom, I have all that on video games. It's the way of the future."

"Hmm. It's not the way of *your* future," his mother said.

Cody looked at his mother's face. When she had that look it usually meant he was in for trouble. Cody rose from the sofa and pointed the remote control at his mother. He pushed the mute button a few times but nothing happened.

"Very funny," she said. "That just shows me how out of touch with reality you are. This," she held up the camp video, "is reality." She pushed the videotape into the VCR and turned it on.

A group of kids in Camp Bear T-shirts came onto the screen. They began to cheer.

"Wadda wadda wooo
Willi willi wear

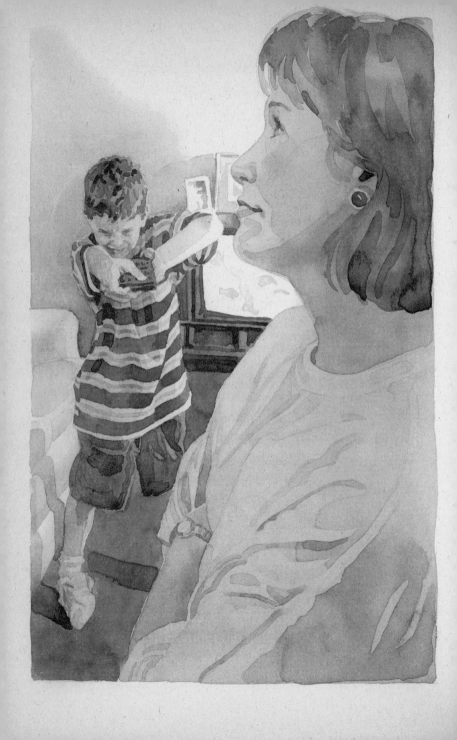

Oomachucka oomachucka
Caaaaaaamp Bear!"

Cody's mother jumped up and down a few
times like a cheerleader at a football game. "I
haven't heard that cheer in years, Cody," she
said. "I'm going to call Camp Bear right now
to see if they have any vacancies."

Cody turned the video off and switched
back to the Road Runner cartoon. It was over.
He turned the TV off and looked at the black
screen. He imagined the anvil falling down
toward Coyote, the look of dread on his face
as the anvil closed in. Then he imagined
Road Runner zipping onto the screen and
coming to a quick stop. But instead of saying "beep beep," Road Runner said "oomachucka oomachucka" as the anvil squashed
Coyote.

His mother ran back into the room. "Good
news, Cody, there was a cancellation so they
have a spot for you."

Cody grasped the remote closer to his chest. He looked at his mother in horror.

She put her hands on her hips and gave him her most serious look. "Cody Michaels, you're about to get unplugged."

Cody's Camp Survival Guide
Excuses Not to Go to Camp

1. You might get eaten by a bear
2. Your mom might clean your room while you're gone
3. Your dog might forget you
4. Your <u>Computer Game</u> magazine might come
5. You might miss <u>Wheel of Fortune</u>

Chapter 2
Camp Scare

"I can't do it." Cody stood in the parking lot of the Danville Mall and looked at the big green bus. CAMP BEAR, it said on the side of the bus.

"Cody, anyone can go a week without electricity," his mother said. "What do you think the pioneers did?"

"You don't understand."

Cody's dad cleared his throat. "Whether you think you can or whether you think you can't you're probably right."

Cody scratched his head. He could never understand what his dad was saying.

His mother was wearing a Camp Bear T-shirt and a Camp Bear cap covered with Camp Bear pins. The T-shirt was faded and a little too small. She had found all of her old camp things in a box in the basement. "I wish I was the one going," she said.

"Me, too," Cody answered looking at the bus. The front of the bus looked like a face. The headlights made two sinister eyes, the grille a scary mouth. The paint on the bus peeled off like skin.

Camp Scare thought Cody.

He had watched the camp video five times. Kids shooting arrows. Kids on horses. Kids hiking in the woods. They looked strong and confident. He did not see anyone on the video who looked like him.

"Co-dy," his mom said. "Let's get a good Camp Bear attitude."

"A journey of a thousand miles begins with a single step," his father added.

A bald man with a clipboard began to read off names and kids got on the bus one by one.

"Junie Andrews," he read.

A girl with red hair yelled, "Here!" then hugged her father and got on the bus.

"Arthur Bonner," the man read.

"Here!" a boy with brown curly hair answered. A woman in a striped dress hugged him good-bye.

"My stomach hurts," Cody said to his parents as he watched the boy get on the bus. "I'd better not go."

Cody thought longingly of his new video game at home, Dragon Quest. You moved up a level each time you overcame one of the dragon's traps. So far he had reached sixteen levels. He could be at home right now with Chip outsmarting the dragon.

"It's going to be fine, Cody. You're going to have a great time at camp."

"When the going gets tough," his dad said, "the tough get going."

"I know," Cody said. "It's just that maybe I should wait a few days and make sure I'm not sick."

"You're not sick," his mom said. "Just a little nervous."

"Matt Lambert," the man called out. His name would be called soon.

"I loved Camp Bear," his mother said. "Didn't I tell you about the time I won the contest for the Izzy Dizzy Race? Here's the pin, right here." She pointed to her hat.

"You told me, Mom."

"The longest lanyard?"

"You told me."

"The most camp spirit?"

"Yeah." Cody looked at his mother and took a step away. She had told him the history behind each of her pins, and when she talked about camp spirit he knew what would happen. Surely she wouldn't do it in the parking lot?

"Mom?"

She was already getting into position, hunched over like she was about to be sick.

"Is your mother okay?" the woman in the striped dress asked him.

"No," he answered. "You'd better cover your ears."

"Wadda wadda wooo
Willi willi wear
Oomachucka oomachucka
Caaaaaaamp Bear!"

She ended in a pose like a grizzly with her arms up over her head.

A few people clapped weakly. Even the man with the clipboard had stopped reading names to stare at her.

She bowed.

"I just remembered, Mom. I haven't finished my summer reading yet. I'd better—"

"You'll have plenty of time for summer reading, Cody," his father said, smiling. "I put one of your summer reading books in your suitcase. Like I always say, Be prepared."

"Oh," said Cody.

"Cody Michaels," the bald man said.

Cody was silent. His mind was churning with too many thoughts. Arrows and poison ivy. Bears and Izzy Dizzy contests. Then he thought about the sofa by the TV, Dragon Quest, Chip, and his dog, Pal. He couldn't say anything.

"Here!" his mother said for him.

His father patted him on the back. As his mother hugged him, her eyes filled with tears.

It was just like a movie he had seen where a mother and father sent their son off to war. The son didn't come back.

Cody looked at the big green bus and took a deep breath.

He remembered a book that he had put in his suitcase. *Wilderness Survival.* Just like his father said, the first rule of survival was to be prepared.

Cody had packed a first-aid kit just like on the list. He had seven pairs of socks. Seven pairs of underwear. Ten T-shirts. A flashlight. A whistle.

He had spent the whole week packing. So why did he feel so unprepared?

Cody's Camp Survival Guide
What to Pack

1. ~~TV~~   Book
2. ~~Microwave~~   Matches
3. ~~Nintendo~~   Deck of Cards
4. ~~Computer~~   Pencil

Chapter 3

Wild Animals

Cody found a seat and sat down. He adjusted his book bag next to him.

"He's sitting down," a girl behind him whispered loudly.

She was talking about *him*.

The bus started with a groan then jerked forward and they were on their way. Cody waved weakly to his father and to his mother, who was hopping up and down outside in the parking lot.

They had taken such good care of him up till this point in his life, and now he didn't know what had gotten into them. Camp was a dangerous place filled with bears and poison ivy. All kinds of bad things could happen. His only experience with bears was Yogi and Boo Boo.

"His name's Cody," another girl whispered. Cody looked at the name tag that his mother had put on the backpack.

She had labeled everything. Even his underwear had little labels with his name ironed inside. That way if he didn't make it out alive at least his parents would get his underwear back.

Cody felt his ears turning red. He took out his book on wilderness survival. He needed to take his mind off the girls and to get ready for all the dangers at camp.

He read a chapter about insects and a chapter about snakes. He turned to a chapter about bears:

Bears are fast and strong and will not hesitate to defend themselves and their

young if they feel threatened. They are
dangerous and can inflict serious damage
or life-threatening injury.

Cody adjusted the book. Fast and strong? Life-threatening injury? All Yogi did was steal picnic baskets. How could his parents do this to him? These were the same parents who wouldn't let him carry a pocketknife or go to the mall alone.

The girls behind him giggled.

"Talk to him," one girl said.

"No, you talk to him," the other one said.

Cody sat and prayed that no one would talk to him. He was still embarrassed by his mother's performance in the parking lot.

What did they want from him anyway?

He tried to keep his mind on the book:

When you hike, make loud noises.
Whistle or sing. Carry a noisemaker.

What kind of noisemaker? One year his mother had brought a noisemaker back from a New Year's Eve party. It had a little crank and you swung it around and around over your head. He couldn't imagine walking through the woods swinging the little crank over his head.

More giggling from behind him.

If you encounter a bear do not run. A bear can run as fast as a racehorse.

This was not good news.

Don't scream or make sudden movements. This can frighten a bear and trigger an attack. Instead, keep calm. Back up slowly. Speak in a calm voice or sing softly.

If caught by the bear don't panic. Do not resist, go limp and cover your head with your arms.

A finger poked him in the back. He turned around to see two girls. He recognized the one with the curly red hair. The other one was dressed all in purple. Even her eyeglasses were purple.

"Hey," the purple girl said. "Junie thinks you're cute."

The redhead giggled.

The book dropped from Cody's fingers. Now he knew what the hikers in the book felt. Panic.

He couldn't back up slowly.

He couldn't speak in a soft comforting voice.

Singing was out of the question. There was only one thing left to do.

Cody laced his fingers behind his head.

Then he put his head down in his lap and went limp.

He had prepared for all sorts of wild creatures, but he had forgotten about the most dangerous kind—the human ones.

Cody's Camp Survival Guide
Concerns for Campers

1. Mosquitoes
2. Ticks
3. Snakes
4. Bears
5. Poison Ivy
6. Wolves
7. Girls

Chapter 4

Moose

Cody rested his head against the window. The girls had settled down and were playing cards behind him.

"Give me all your twos," one was saying.

Cody just kept watching the world pass by. First towns, buildings, stores, parking lots, then neighborhoods and houses.

He was moving farther and farther from his home. For a while he tried to memorize the way they were going, but he realized it was hopeless.

He remembered reading "Hansel and Gretel" when he was little, and how Hansel had dropped bread crumbs in the forest to mark his way. He found some M&M's in his backpack. Should he drop them out the window?

Then he remembered that birds had eaten the bread crumbs in the story. He could imagine a ferocious grizzly eating the M&M's one by one and following the trail not to his house but to him! He closed the bag of M&M's.

There was no way that he could get back on his own. Now they were traveling through forests and the light was dim, the road shaded by trees. When he looked out into the forest he could see nothing but trees and more trees.

"That's where the bears are," a voice said beside him. The voice was deep and gruff like a man's.

Cody looked up to see a large muscular boy staring down at him. He looked like one of the campers in Cody's video, strong and self-assured.

"There aren't any bears up here," Cody said, but his voice cracked.

"Sure," the boy said. "I bet that's what your mommy told you."

Cody looked back out the window. The forest *did* look like a place where bears would live.

The boy moved over and sat beside him. He had a Camp Bear cap like Cody's mother, and like hers it was covered with pins. Cody wondered if he would ever have pins like that.

"I'm Moose," the boy said.

Cody had seen a moose once on TV. It was big and strong like the boy. But it also had a goofy kind of face like the boy. It was a good nickname. He thought about what kind of animal he could be named for but all he could think of was Mouse.

"I'm Cody," he said.

"That's where the wolves live," Moose said as they passed a mountain.

Cody didn't answer. He didn't know whether to believe Moose or not. The mountain definitely looked dark and scary.

26

The bus creaked as they turned off of the highway and onto a dirt road. Cody could see the sign for Camp Bear as they passed under it. He remembered his mother's words: *You'll be just fine.*

He kept telling himself that as they drove past an old cabin and a few totem poles.

He would be just fine.

They passed a lake. It was covered with green scummy stuff.

He would be just fine.

"Look to the left," the man with the clipboard said. "You'll see the lake. We'll meet there after you check in."

Why were they meeting there? Cody wondered.

"Wear your swimsuit and bring your towel."

Swimsuit? Towel?

He thought of the swimming pool near his house. It was clear, clean water and yet his mother always worried whether the water was clean enough. The lifeguards tested it every hour for cleanliness with a little chemical kit. What was she thinking sending him up here in the wilderness to swim in scum?

"They always have a swim test the first day," Moose said. "If the snakes don't get you then you pass."

This time Cody believed him.

Would he be just fine?

Cody's Camp Survival Guide
Kids to Avoid at Camp

1. Kids who wet the bed and sleep on the top bunk
2. Kids who wear nose plugs while swimming
3. Kids who have the name of an animal
4. Kids who have no pins

Chapter 5

Swimming Bare?

A teenager with a clipboard came into the cabin and sat down on the bed across from Cody. "Cody, right?" he asked. Cody nodded. "Hi," he said. "I'm your counselor, Running Dog."

"Running Dog?"

"That's my Indian name," he said. "You can also call me Jim."

"Does everyone have a nickname?" Cody asked.

"Not a nickname," said Jim. "A Native American name. You'll have one before the day is out. It's a Camp Bear tradition. But we

can't just give you any name. First we have to
see what you're like. You have to earn your
name."

Cody held his breath. What could his
Indian name be? It was like the first day of
school—a good nickname could make or break
your whole year. His had almost been ruined
last year when he had been Cootie. What
could he do to earn his Indian name?

He imagined rescuing a girl from a burn-
ing cabin. He would emerge from the flames
with the girl in his arms. Everyone would
gather around. "You will no longer be known
as Cody," someone would say. "You are now
Fire Walker."

He couldn't wait to get his new name.

Jim helped Cody put his trunk behind the
end of one of the bunk beds. "Get changed
and head down to the lake for the swim test.
You've got about ten minutes."

Cody imagined swimming swiftly across
the lake.

You will no longer be known as Cody. You are

now *Swimming Shark*. Did Indians know about sharks?

Then he remembered the lake scum. *You are now Swimming Scum.*

"Do I have to?" he asked.

"Yeah." Jim stood up and headed to the door. "You have to pass a swim test before you can do any of the water activities. No way out."

Cody got out his *Wilderness Survival* book and read the section on water safety. Watch out for the "dangerous toos," it said: too tired, too cold, too far from safety. He added his own: too scummy.

The boy with curly hair from the bus walked in and dropped a backpack on the bunk beside Cody.

"Hi, my name's Arthur," he said.

"I'm Cody."

"Hey, you." Moose walked in carrying his sleeping bag. He frowned at Cody. "That's my lucky bed."

"What's so lucky about this bed?" Cody asked.

"Us experienced guys know that the bed by the door is the best for watching out."

"Watching out for what?"

"If any other cabins try to attack us or anything, I'll be here to take care of it."

"Okay," Cody said. He didn't mind the idea of being protected. He moved his trunk to the bunk where Arthur was unrolling his sleeping bag.

"You been to camp before?" Cody asked Arthur. Arthur shook his head.

"It's my first year," he said miserably. "My folks went to Europe."

"That's terrible," Cody said. "They went on vacation without you?"

Arthur nodded.

"Great," said Moose, "I'm stuck with two rookies." He smoothed out his sleeping bag. Cody noticed a lump at the bottom. "Remember, rookies, nobody touches my stuff. Got it?"

Arthur and Cody nodded. "What's in your

sleeping bag?" Cody asked Moose. Moose's eyes narrowed. "MYOB," he said gruffly as he walked out for the swim test.

"What does that mean?" Cody asked Arthur.

"Mind your own business," Arthur said.

Cody looked one more time at the lump. "Sorry I asked," he said. Arthur giggled.

"Let's move it guys," Jim called from outside. "Time for the swim test."

Cody opened his trunk and found his swimsuit. His mother had packed a blue one with white polka dots that he hated. He looked for the string to tie the waist but it was gone.

"What's the matter?" Arthur asked.

"No string."

"I have a safety pin."

Cody pinned the waist of the swimsuit. It seemed to stay up just fine.

Cody and Arthur hurried down the path to the lake. There was a crowd at the lake for the swim test. Kids stood on the wooden dock or sat on towels in the grass. Cody recognized Junie and the other girl from the bus standing on the dock. Moose and Jim were there, too.

Cody and Arthur hurried to the dock and got in line behind Moose.

Three kids were already lined up at the end of the dock. Mr. Major, the bald guy from the bus, blew the whistle and the kids dove in and swam toward a buoy. They swam around the buoy and swam back. When they got out of the water they were covered with bits of green slime.

Mr. Major marked their times down as they got out of the water. "Passed," he said.

Cody looked at the lake and the buoy. He wasn't a great swimmer but he could make it across the lake and back.

"Next," Mr. Major said.

Cody, Moose, and Arthur stepped up to the edge of the dock.

The whistle blew. They jumped. Cody hit the water with a loud smack, stung by the cold. Moose took off cutting the water with sharp, crisp strokes. Arthur swam fast. Cody treaded water for a second, then began to paddle toward the rope. Green stuff clung to his shoulders and he had the feeling it was on his head, too. Seaweed tendrils wrapped around his leg.

Slowly he paddled forward. He thought of his father's saying: Slow and steady wins the race. Moose swam by him going the other way. Arthur followed. Cody just kept going toward the buoy.

Hand over hand like his swim instructor at the Y had taught him. He was doing great. His feet kicked out behind him like a pair of scissors. His arms moved like a windmill.

He knew he could make it. When he reached the buoy he turned around and started back. He kicked even harder. He touched the edge of the dock and then raised his fist in a victory sign. "Passed!" Mr. Major said. He had made it!

That's when Junie screamed and pointed to the lake. There was something blue floating on the water. It had white polka dots. It looked exactly like his swimsuit.

"Your suit!" Arthur yelled.

Cody suddenly felt very cold. Now he was happy for the green scum. Jim dove in to rescue the suit.

Cody clung to the dock carefully, trying not to disturb any of the lake scum that was shielding him.

Moose stood on the dock and laughed. Junie giggled from the dock, "He's swimming bare," she said.

Moose called out to Cody. "Hey, I just thought of something!"

"What?" Cody asked as he watched Jim swim toward him with the polka-dot suit.

"Your new Indian name."

"What?"

"You will no longer be known as Cody. You are now . . ." He paused. "Swimming Bare."

Cody's Camp Survival Guide
The Dangerous Toos

Before swimming make sure to check these
dangerous toos:
1. Too cold?
2. Too far from safety?
3. Too tired?
4. Too scummy?
5. Swimsuit too loose?

Chapter 6

The Haunted Hamster

"Is Tweety a boy or a girl?"

The boys of Cabin Nine sat together at the campfire. There were Arthur, Moose, and Cody, and the twins that everyone called Mike and Ike because they were always eating candy. The entire camp circled the ring of fire. Each cabin had their own log to sit on.

Cabin Nine was playing TV trivia. Cody was good. "Tweety's a boy!" he said. He thought of a new question. "How many dogs have the Simpsons had?"

Everyone thought.

"Two?" Moose said.

"Nope."

"Fourteen?" Mike guessed.

Arthur was quiet, thinking hard. "I think I've got it," he said finally. "Twenty-eight."

"Right!" Everyone clapped. Cody couldn't believe there was someone else there who knew as much as he did about TV.

Cody could see Junie and Kay sitting on a log across from them. Kay wore a purple jacket. Her Indian name was Sitting Plum.

By now they all had their Indian names. Arthur got his at the swim test, too, but he had come out better than Cody: Little Otter. Now everyone called him Otter.

The twins were Walks-with-Milk-Duds and Snickers-Boy. Moose had gotten his name last year: Eats-Like-Moose.

The fire looked eerie. A shower of sparks shot up and blew away into the night.

In the distance they heard the soft beating of a drum. Everyone got quiet. As the drum seemed to get closer and closer, the only other sound was the pop of the fire. A voice was chanting solemnly in time to the beat of the drum.

"It's Mr. Major," Moose whispered. "He does this every year."

"Shhh," Cody said. He didn't want to know the details. It was like hearing the end of a TV show before you saw it.

As they watched, a man dressed in buckskins and a feathered headdress danced into the campfire circle. Did he look a little like Mr. Major?

The lone man circled the fire three times while beating the tom-tom, then hit the drum hard once, and stopped. Cody drew in his breath.

"Long ago," he began, "on Bear Mountain . . . there was a young brave. Like all of the young braves he had to undergo tests of courage—tests to prove that he was a man."

Cody watched the lone man standing in the glow of the campfire. The chief raised a stick into the air. It had feathers attached to the end.

"As the young brave completed each feat of bravery he carved a notch in his courage stick."

Now Cody could make out notches carved along the stick. "When his stick was filled with notches . . . then he was a man."

He lifted the stick above his head. "I challenge you boys and girls at Camp Bear to try new things this week. To be brave."

The chief began dancing to the rhythm of the tom-tom once again. Then he left the circle and vanished into the darkness.

Jim got up and stood before the fire. "Chief Oomachucka has spoken," he said. "The week begins."

They all sang "Kum ba ya" then walked back to the cabins in the dark. Their flashlights lit the woods and made scary shapes in the trees. Cody walked close to Otter. Moose and Mike and Ike walked behind them.

"Scared?" Moose asked.

"I'm not scared," Cody said, but he looked uneasily at the dark woods ahead.

"We haven't even started the ghost stories yet," said Moose. "That will come later."

"Ghost stories?" Otter said.

"Yeah, rookies. Ghost stories."

"I don't know," said Cody. "I think it might be too late." He had made it a point never to watch scary things after dark. Once he had watched the previews for a movie called *Night of the Vampires* and had had to sleep on the floor of his parents' bedroom in a sleeping bag.

The movie had been set in the forest. The tree branches had been black and scary and had blown in the wind. Crickets had been peeping and frogs had croaked. But when the vampire moved through the forest, the crickets and frogs became silent.

A twig snapped. Cody jumped. His flashlight beam lit on a stick at the edge of the path. Cody picked it up. A courage stick—also handy for hitting vampires on the head.

"It's never too late for scary stories," said Moose.

Cody looked at the black curvy branches of the trees that blew in the wind. Crickets were peeping and frogs were croaking. He hoped that the peeping and croaking would not stop.

They finally got to the cabin and settled in for the night. The boys pulled their sleeping bags into a circle on the floor.

Moose put his flashlight up to his face and made a scary face.

Cody felt a chill go down his back. He snuggled as far down into his sleeping bag as he could go. He tried to think of some of his father's sayings to make himself feel better. *You have nothing to fear but fear itself.* It didn't help. He tried not to listen but he couldn't help it.

Moose began. "Once there was a boy who had a hamster named Hairy. Hairy was a happy hamster. He would run on his wheel every night: *creak, creak, creak.* The wheel needed oil."

Moose talked in a low voice. Cody could

imagine the hamster running on the wheel. In his mind the hamster was not small and fuzzy like the one in his classroom last year. Instead Hairy was wicked looking with long fangs and green glowing eyes.

"Hairy would sleep every day and run on the wheel every night. *Creak. Creak. Creak.* One day there was a terrible accident. Hairy escaped from his cage, and as he hurried across the boy's bedroom floor, Pogo the cat pounced. Hairy was no more . . . or so everyone thought."

Cody gripped his courage stick.

"The next night when the boy went to bed he heard *creak, creak, creak.* He looked up and saw the hamster wheel turning. But Hairy wasn't there. . . ."

Cody gasped.

"Lights out!" a voice called, and the flashlights went out. They pulled their sleeping bags back to their beds and everyone was quiet.

Soon Cody heard the other boys snoring,

but he couldn't go to sleep. He just lay there thinking.

As far as he could make out, camp was like a giant unplugged video game. Earning a pin was like moving up a level in the game. But instead of doing things that were possible, like zapping aliens and gnomes, you had to do things that were impossible: winning swimming races in scummy ponds or hitting the bull's-eye with an arrow. Instead of avoiding things like magic mountains and flying monkeys, you had to watch out for dangers that were real: bears and poison ivy.

Cody took out his stick and his pocketknife and carved one small notch in the stick. He had not earned any pins but he had still overcome a lot of challenges. He would mark off each level he passed, just like in Dragon Quest. Only this would be Camp Quest.

The first notch was for coming to camp. Then he carved a second notch, for surviving the girls on the bus. Then a third, for jumping into the scummy lake and passing the swim test. And a fourth: he had listened to a ghost story. And a fifth: he looked at Otter's leg hanging down from the top bunk. He had made a friend. He put his knife and stick away. The morning in the parking lot felt like it took place weeks instead of hours ago. When he thought of all the notches on his stick he felt better.

But what would his challenges be *tomorrow*?

Cody's Camp Survival Guide

Camp Names You Want	Camp Names You Don't Want
1. Strength-of-Buffalo	1. Breath-of-Buffalo
2. Running Deer	2. Running Nose
3. Eagle Boy	3. Chicken Boy
4. Strong-Like-Moose	4. Eats-Like-Moose
5. Brave Bear	5. Swimming Bare

Chapter 7

"Squeak!"

Creak. Creak. Creak.

Cody's eyes popped open. He sat up in his bunk bed so fast that he almost fell out.

He looked around the small cabin. The creak was coming from the old screened door of the cabin. Mike and Ike were already dressed and heading out for breakfast.

Cody sank back down on the bed. He thought about Moose's ghost story. It didn't seem so scary now. A haunted hamster seemed funny.

Creak. Creak. Creak.

How could he ever have thought that was scary? Outside the window the branches of the trees were covered with bright green leaves and the sky was blue.

A trumpet sounded a peppy wake-up call in the distance and he was filled with optimism. He was at camp and the first full day was about to begin. A new beginning.

Otter called from the top bunk. "What's the name of the lunch lady on the Simpsons?"

Cody looked up over the bed. "Doris," he said.

"Where does Wile E. Coyote get his stuff?" Cody asked.

"Acme."

"Rise and shine," Jim called out. "Up and at 'em."

Cody pulled out a clean T-shirt and shorts and got dressed. He looked over at Otter. Otter was poking the bottom of Moose's sleeping bag. "There's definitely something in here," he said.

Cody felt a ripple of fear go through him.

"Don't touch that," he said. "Moose will kill us."

Jim poked his head through the screened door. "Come on," he said. They hurried out to the dining hall for breakfast.

The cook placed a half moon of eggs on Cody's plate with an ice-cream scoop. The eggs stayed in the shape of the little dome. Some egg water oozed out from it and ran across his plate.

"Gross," Otter said.

"Disgusting," Cody said. He moved his biscuit so it wouldn't get wet.

They went through the line and found a seat. Junie and Kay sat down across the table from them. Kay had on a purple T-shirt and a purple hair ribbon.

"Hi," Junie said. "We could starve with this food." Kay just smiled.

Cody pulled his survival guide from his pocket and read from it. "Did you know that starvation in the woods is next to impossible?" he asked.

"They've never eaten at Camp Bear," Moose said as he sat down with them. Junie laughed.

"Listen," Cody said. "Insects are the perfect food source, providing more energy than fish or meat. They are mostly fat."

"My mother always said I should eat a low-fat diet," said Junie. "Besides, eating bugs is mean."

Cody looked up at her. "Why, do you like bugs?" he asked.

"Yeah," she said, "but not to eat."

Cody noticed that Junie looked a little bit like Holly, a girl in his class at school. Holly was nice, for a girl, and she liked bugs, too.

Otter tried to cut his biscuit, but only made a small dent in it with his knife. "I think these biscuits are leftovers," he said.

"Yeah," Moose said, "from last year."

"Grasshoppers are a delicacy in many countries," Cody read. "Remove wings and legs and toast the body on a stick."

"Gross," Kay said. "Read more."

"You can make ant lemonade by mashing them in water sweetened by berries or tree sap." He looked at the thick juice in his glass. "I don't think I'm thirsty."

"Here, rookies." Moose picked up a biscuit. "This is how you do it." He turned the biscuit to its side, took his knife, and drilled a hold into the middle of the biscuit. Then he took the maple syrup from the center of the table and began to fill up the hole. When it was full he put the biscuit down.

"There," he said. "That softens it up." He popped the biscuit into his mouth. Syrup dripped down his chin.

"Good idea," Cody said. "Sometimes survival is being creative."

Cody and Otter began drilling their biscuits. Cody watched Moose as he drilled another biscuit. Moose knew everything. It must feel good to be so confident.

"What will we do today?" Cody asked Otter.

"We could go to archery."

Cody remembered a Road Runner cartoon where Coyote had shot an arrow. The arrow hit the side of a hill that was shaped like a curve. Then the arrow had turned and chased him.

"I don't think so," Cody said.

"We're going water skiing," the girls said.

Cody thought about his swimsuit and shook his head.

Otter looked up. "How about arts and crafts?"

Cody smiled. What could be safer than arts and crafts?

"Arts and crafts it is," Cody said. That was the one thing they could do and not get into trouble.

Otter smiled and bit into his biscuit. Syrup oozed down his chin like Moose's.

Moose looked up from his biscuit. "Manly men go horseback riding," he said. "Mousely men go to arts and crafts."

Cody thought for a moment. Horses were

big. Should he be a manly man like Moose or a mousely man like himself?

He thought about horses he had seen on TV. They always seem to be rearing up on their hind legs or galloping fast.

"Are you a man," said Moose, "or a mouse?"

Cody and Otter answered together. "Squeak!"

Cody's Camp Survival Guide
Surviving Camp Food

1. Rub leftovers on your body for insect repellent
2. Be sure to say grace before the meal
3. Say grace during the meal
4. Say grace after the meal if you live
5. If it moves, don't eat it

Chapter 8

Throwing Pots

Cody looked at the lump of clay in front of him. It looked slimy. He had a hard time thinking of it as a bowl. He pounded it with his fist. Then he began to knead it like dough, just the way Jim had shown them.

"Good," Jim said. "First we need to get all the bubbles out."

Cody watched the other kids pounding their clay. Otter was rolling his clay like a long snake. He was glad that he wasn't on a horse or shooting arrows. This was fun and a safe choice of activities.

Cody patted his clay ball down and pressed it some more.

"What do you think about Moose?" Otter asked.

Cody pounded his clay a few times before answering. "You know how every cartoon has a bad guy?"

"Like Roger on *Doug's Place* or Angelica on *Rug Rats?*"

"Yeah, well Moose is the bad guy."

Otter was coiling his clay snake into a bowl. Cody's ball of clay was on the wheel.

"What do you think it is?" Otter asked.

"What?"

"The lump in Moose's sleeping bag."

"I don't know. Candy?"

Otter shook his head. "No, Moose's trunk is filled with candy. He left most of his clothes home so that he could fit all that candy in. I don't think he would hide it in his sleeping bag."

"Weapons?"

Otter shrugged. "I hope not."

Cody tried to imagine what kind of lumpy weapons Moose could have. Water balloons and toilet paper were all he could come up with.

"I don't think he would hide weapons," Cody said.

"We'll just have to find out for ourselves."

"What do you mean?"

"I mean we'll have to look and see," Otter said.

"Moose will kill us."

"Moose won't know. We'll divert his attention, then sneak in and look."

Cody felt a ripple of excitement, like when he started a new level on his video games. A mission: to find out what was in Moose's sleeping bag. It would be dangerous, but something about the danger appealed to him.

"We'll do it," he said.

"Okay," Jim called out, "let's start the wheels. I'll show you how to throw a pot."

Cody followed Jim's instructions.

He centered the lump of clay on the wheel.

He put his feet on the foot wheel and gave it a little kick. The pottery wheel spun around. "Careful," said Jim. "Not too fast."

Otter kicked his. "Cool," he said. He stuck his finger into the clay and made a hole in the center.

"The most important thing is to keep it in the center," said Jim. "And keep it slow."

Cody put his hands around the spinning clay. He could control the shape by moving his hands. He imagined the pot that he would make. It would be beautiful. He would win the prize for the best pot ever made at Camp Bear. He looked down at the lump of clay spinning on the wheel. It was perfect.

Two faces appeared at the screened window. Junie and Kay.

The girls giggled. "Can we watch?"

"Sure," Cody said. "Come on in." He was nervous but pleased to have an audience. He concentrated even harder on making the clay into a bowl. He pressed his fingers inside and the sides of the bowl grew.

"Wow," Junie said. "You're good at that."

Cody felt his confidence rise.

"I've always been good at art," he said. "I illustrated all the posters for my school talent show."

"Cool," Junie said. Her tiny gold earrings sparkled.

Cody forgot to look at his pot. He could only look at Junie.

Kay grinned. "Junie wants to know if you'll dance with her at the dance Friday night."

He kicked once too hard.

The wheel kept spinning and the clay took off so quickly that Cody couldn't catch it. Pieces of the clay flew everywhere. Junie and Kay put their hands up to protect themselves but a spattering of gray blobs covered them.

Cody stared blankly at the empty wheel spinning in front of him. One minute he was making the best pot in the history of Camp Bear, the next minute it had turned into a weapon.

He looked at the clay splattered every-

60

where. He looked at the surprised faces of the girls. Then he thought of his courage stick. Survival meant trying again.

"Excuse me," he said to the girls. Junie and Kay started to laugh. Otter and Cody laughed with them. He picked up another ball of clay and started to pound it.

Cody's Camp Survival Guide
Safe Places at Camp

1. ???

Chapter 9

Moose Survival

Cody's courage stick began to fill with notches. There was one for eating camp food, and one for surviving arts and crafts. One for taking a shower with a daddy longlegs, and another for cleaning a fish that he caught.

As the days flew by, one challenge followed another, but the biggest challenge was still before him: finding out what was in the bottom of Moose's sleeping bag. He and Otter had already made two attempts on the sleeping bag, but both had been unsuccessful.

The first try had been frightening. Cody and Otter had crept over to Moose's bunk while he was in the shower. They had heard the water running and knew that when it stopped Moose would be coming back.

Cody had reached all the way down, and his hand had actually brushed against the hidden object when the water stopped.

In his rush to get away he had tripped over his trunk and collided with Otter.

They had been lying in a pile on the cabin floor when Moose walked in from the shower. He stood looking at them for a moment.

"You guys aren't bothering my stuff are you?"

"Ah, why would we do that Moose?" said Cody.

"You don't want to live long maybe?"

The second attempt had taken place while Moose was horseback riding.

Cody and Otter came back early from their nature hike. Otter went in and Cody kept watch. As he stood guard in front of the cabin, he remembered a trick from his survival guide that would alert them to Moose's approach.

In the book it said to cup your hand over your ear and press it to the ground. Cody cupped his hand over his ear and pressed it to the ground. No sounds. They were safe.

He imagined that he was a brave and he was listening for buffalo. He needed to protect his tribe from stampede.

"Hey, you talking to worms?" It was Moose. He hadn't heard him come down the path!

"Hey MOOSE!" he said loudly to warn Otter.

"You don't have to yell."

"Just trying out my vocal cords, MOOSE!"

Otter hurried out of the cabin. He looked guilty.

Moose went into the cabin.

"That was close," Cody said.

"Too close."

"Did you see it?"

Otter shook his head. No luck.

The next day Cody and Otter finished a canoe trip early. "Nice job, guys," Jim said.

"You've got some free time. Anything else you want to do?"

Cody looked at Otter, Otter looked back. "I think we'll just go back to the cabin for a little while before lunch," Cody said.

Otter and Cody crept toward their cabin.

Cody felt like he was in a James Bond movie—sneaking into a highly dangerous situation. They walked down the path looking in all directions. The coast was clear. They walked through the door, checking right and left. The coast was clear. They looked around the small room and under the beds. The coast was clear.

Finally they stood in front of Moose's bed. Cody touched the lump from the outside.

"Here goes," he said. He slowly unzipped the sleeping bag. He pulled out a gym bag. Cody unzipped the gym bag. Otter let out a gasp as the contents were revealed.

"Wow."

"Incredible."

Cody picked up a small teddy bear that

had been hidden in the bottom of Moose's sleeping bag. "Moose has a teddy bear."

Cody sat down and studied the teddy bear. It was so old its eyes were gone and its fur was worn off in spots.

"Moose has a teddy?" Otter repeated.

Cody could only nod his head.

"What should we do? We could put it up the flagpole."

Cody shook his head. "No, even Moose doesn't deserve that."

"You're right," Otter said.

Very slowly and carefully they put the teddy bear back in the gym bag. Very slowly and carefully they put the gym bag back down inside the sleeping bag and zipped it up.

"I sort of wish we hadn't looked," Cody said.

"Me too," Otter replied.

Cody looked at the lump on the bed with new eyes.

Moose was just trying to survive, too.

Cody's Camp Survival Guide
The Rule of Three

1. You can survive three minutes without air
2. You can survive three days without water
3. You can survive three weeks without food
4. You can't survive three nights without your teddy bear

Chapter 10

Manly Men

"Which T-shirt looks better," Otter asked, "the Mighty Ducks or the Atlanta Braves?" He held up two shirts for Cody to choose from. It had been a long week, and the T-shirts showed it. They had made crafts and hiked, paddled canoes and played basketball. Tonight was the dance, tomorrow was the overnight camp-out at Bear Mountain, then the next day they would go home.

"The Atlanta Braves smells better," Cody responded.

"Good thinking," Otter said. He put on the

T-shirt and tossed the Mighty Ducks under the bed.

"So," he said to Cody, "have you ever been to a dance?"

Cody shook his head. Every time he thought about dancing his stomach grew tight.

Moose came in. "You guys scared of girls?" he asked. "Manly men are not afraid of anything."

Cody looked at Otter and winked. "Right, Moose."

After dinner, Cabin Nine walked to the dance together. The dance was held around a campfire. Mr. Major had brought a small boom box that played CDs. They were very old CDs.

Cody listened to the music for a while. He watched the other dancers. Everyone had a unique style of dancing.

Moose danced chicken style: his arms flapped up and down like wings and his feet moved like a chicken scratching in the dirt.

Otter had an exercise style. It looked like he was doing jumping jacks. Mike and Ike had an air-guitar style. They jumped up and down swinging one arm in a circle as if they were holding guitars.

Even Mr. Major danced. He reminded Cody of a lumbering grizzly bear.

Cody couldn't move. He wasn't exactly sure how to do it. He would just have to watch a while until he caught on a little bit. He noticed what a good dancer Junie was, but how could he ask her to dance if he didn't know how?

Just then Junie walked up to him.

"Cody would you like to dance?"

Cody opened and closed his mouth a few times like a fish. He couldn't speak. All at once he heard Moose laugh behind him, and something small and wiggly dropped down his back.

"EEE!" he called out and started jumping up and down. "All right!" Junie said, and started dancing.

Cody shook his shoulders to the right. The bug crawled up to his neck.

Junie shook her shoulders to the right.

Cody shook his shoulders to the left. The bug crawled down his back.

Junie shook her shoulders to the left.

Cody jumped and wiggled.

Junie jumped and wiggled.

Everyone from the camp gathered around and began to clap. They were a hit.

Cody dropped down to the ground and flopped around on the dirt. Everyone else dropped down, too. "Cool move," said Otter. Cody rubbed his back in the ground and kicked up his feet.

Finally a big brown beetle crawled out, but Cody kept going. He could dance after all.

"I should be mad, Moose," Cody said when the music stopped.

"Hey," Moose said. "I was just looking out for my friend."

Cody laughed. Moose and Otter laughed.

The music started again, and this time Cody didn't hesitate. He danced every dance.

Cody's Camp Survival Guide
Camp Jokes

1. Put Saran Wrap on the toilet seat
2. Put whipped cream on someone's hand while they are asleep then tickle their nose
3. Put toilet paper anywhere
4. Put a beetle down someone's back

Chapter 11

Wow!

"Up and at 'em, guys," Jim called out. "We've got a big day. It's the hike up Bear Mountain."

Five pillows hit Jim.

"Okay, okay," Jim said. "Wake up and listen. We'll be hiking five miles through the wilderness."

Cody felt a shiver go down his back. Who knew what dangers they would encounter along the way?

"Let's get our packs loaded and our sleeping bags rolled up and ready."

As Cody loaded his backpack, he tried to think of the things they would need.

"What should we bring?" he asked the other guys.

"Water," Otter said as he put the water bottle in his pack.

"M&M's," Mike said.

"Skittles," Ike said.

Moose held up a small black plastic snakebite kit. "I bet we'll need this," he said as he put the plastic case into the pack.

"Stop trying to scare us, Moose," Otter said.

Cody put his wilderness survival guide into his backpack.

"Be prepared," Otter said.

"Right," Cody answered.

"Be prepared," Mike said as he loaded up a bag of Reese's Pieces.

"Right," said Ike as he loaded a pack of Sweetarts.

"Forward ho," Jim called as the campers set out for Bear Mountain.

They passed the lake and the archery field.

They started up the mountain. As they hiked away from camp, the path narrowed and the woods got thicker. The trees blocked the sunlight and the woods were cool and green.

They saw deer tracks and a squirrel's nest.

"Break," Jim said as they entered a small clearing. They stopped and began to set down their backpacks. Jim walked on a little farther to check out the trail.

The boys looked around the clearing. Mike and Ike passed out Sweetarts and Reese's Pieces.

Suddenly Otter stopped. "What's that noise?" he asked.

Cody listened for a moment. He heard a whirring coming from the weeds at the side of the path. Mike and Ike stepped back, but Moose stepped forward. "Let's see," he said, and he reached down to part the tall grass.

"Stop," Cody yelled. The grass shook a little.

Cody grabbed Moose by the arm and

slowly backed him up. Cody's heart thumped. He tried to control the tremor in his voice. He knew what was in the grass. "It's a rattlesnake," he said when he got his breath.

He remembered the chapter about snakes in his survival guide. "Usually snakes will avoid people," he said. "If you surprise a snake it may attack. Avoid contact. Back up slowly."

Jim came up behind them.

"What's up?" he said.

"Listen," said Cody.

They heard the whirring again. Jim got his walking stick and slowly parted the grass. All at once a large rattlesnake bit into the wood and coiled around the stick. They could see the diamond patterns on its body and the rattles of its tail.

The rattler's teeth were embedded in the wood.

Moose gasped. Mike and Ike were speechless.

"Anyone have a pocket knife?" Jim asked calmly.

Cody pulled his out of his pocket and opened it for Jim. Jim cut the snake's head off with one swift movement.

The body writhed on the ground and the head stayed attached to the stick by its sharp fangs.

"Wow," said Moose.

"Wow," said Otter.

By this time, the other campers had been drawn to them by the activity. They all stood in silence and watched the snake's body still twitching on the ground.

"How did you know what to do?" Otter asked Cody.

"My survival guide," Cody said. "I guess it really is good to be prepared."

"I wish I had a video of that," Otter said.

Cody laughed. "Sometimes the real thing is better than any video," he said.

Later that night they lay with their sleeping

bags pulled in a circle. The stars overhead were brighter than Cody had ever imagined stars could be.

This time instead of TV trivia they played camp trivia.

"Most doughnuts eaten in one sitting?"

"Fourteen, by Moose."

"Number of spiders found in Cabin Nine?"

"Twelve."

"Most heroic act?"

"Cody saving Moose from the snake."

Once in a while someone would say, "Wow, that was some snake." And everyone would agree.

Cody's Camp Survival Guide
You know you've been at camp too long when:

1. You start looking forward to the food

2. Your mosquito bites have mosquito bites
3. You accidentally call your counselor Mom
4. You sing "Kum ba ya" in your sleep
5. You start saying, "Wow, that was some snake"

Chapter 12

Going Home

The rest of the camp-out was uneventful. In the morning, they hiked down the mountain and gathered their things for the ride home.

Cody pressed his face against the window of the bus waiting to see his parents in the parking lot. The bus creaked along and eased to a stop beside a small group of parents waiting there.

Cody sat beside Otter, with Moose behind them. His throat was sore from singing camp songs, and he was exhausted from the hike and the camp-out. It had been a great week.

His cap was no longer empty—he had

three new shiny pins. One for most improved camper. One for making the best pot. And one for camp spirit. The pins were great, but when he thought of his stick and the notches in it he was proud.

Before camp he had had a few moments of bravery. There was the time he had just moved to a new school. It had been terrifying to walk into the classroom for the first time. But he had done it.

There was the time when he told everyone that he was a roller-skating champion and he couldn't even skate. But he had put on skates and actually skated, and he had survived.

There was the time he had received a letter from a secret admirer. He didn't even want to think about how terrifying that was. But everything had turned out just fine in the end.

And the time he had to appear in the school talent show and he didn't have a talent. He had survived again.

He thought back on the week now. Camp had been frightening at first. But the fear had been in his own mind, and that kind of fear can be worse than encountering a real danger, like the rattlesnake.

Cody spotted his mother first. She had worn her Camp Bear T-shirt again. "There's my mom." He pointed her out to Otter.

"There's mine," Otter said as he waved out the window.

Cody saw his dad. He was waving the remote control in the air as a welcome-back gesture.

The bus stopped and all the kids ran down the steps.

Cody wrapped his arms around his mom and dad together in a giant group hug.

"How was it?" his mom asked. He could only answer in one word.

"Wow!"

"Look what I brought you," his dad said as he held up the remote. "I know you must have missed this."

"Thanks, Dad," he said. "But I didn't miss it so much after all."

He gave his dad another hug.

Otter came over and gave Cody a high five. "Bye, Cody," he said. Moose joined them and hunched down beside Cody. "Camp cheer!" he called out. Junie ran over. So did Kay.

"Come on, Mom," Cody said.

Cody's mother got in the circle with them. He was glad his mother was just the way she was. He was especially glad that she had made him go to camp.

Life without electricity had been great.

"Wadda wadda wooo
Willi willi wear
Oomachucka oomachucka
Caaaaaaamp Bear!"

Cody's Camp Survival Guide
Things to Remember

1. Kids with animal nicknames can be nice
2. Have a good camp attitude even at meals
3. Don't be afraid to try new things
4. Real life is even better than TV

Betsy Duffey is the author of a wide range of fiction for Viking, including *How to Be Cool in the Third Grade* and *Utterly Yours, Booker Jones*, plus four previous books about Cody: *Hey, New Kid!*, *Virtual Cody*, *Cody's Secret Admirer*, and *Spotlight on Cody*. She lives in Atlanta, Georgia, with her husband and two sons.

Ellen Thompson is the illustrator of all of the Cody books by Betsy Duffey, and has illustrated well over a hundred children's book jackets. Her work has also appeared in numerous magazines. She lives in Franklin Park, New Jersey.

AUG - - 2001

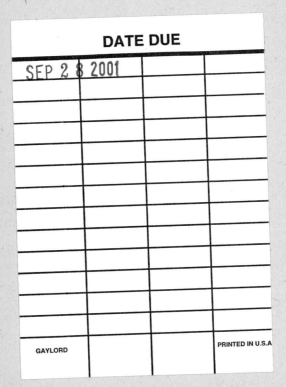

DATE DUE

SEP 2 8 2001			
GAYLORD			PRINTED IN U.S.A